The Man in the Moon

By Diane Brookes

Illustrated by Ann Timmins

Raven Rock Publishing, Yellowknife

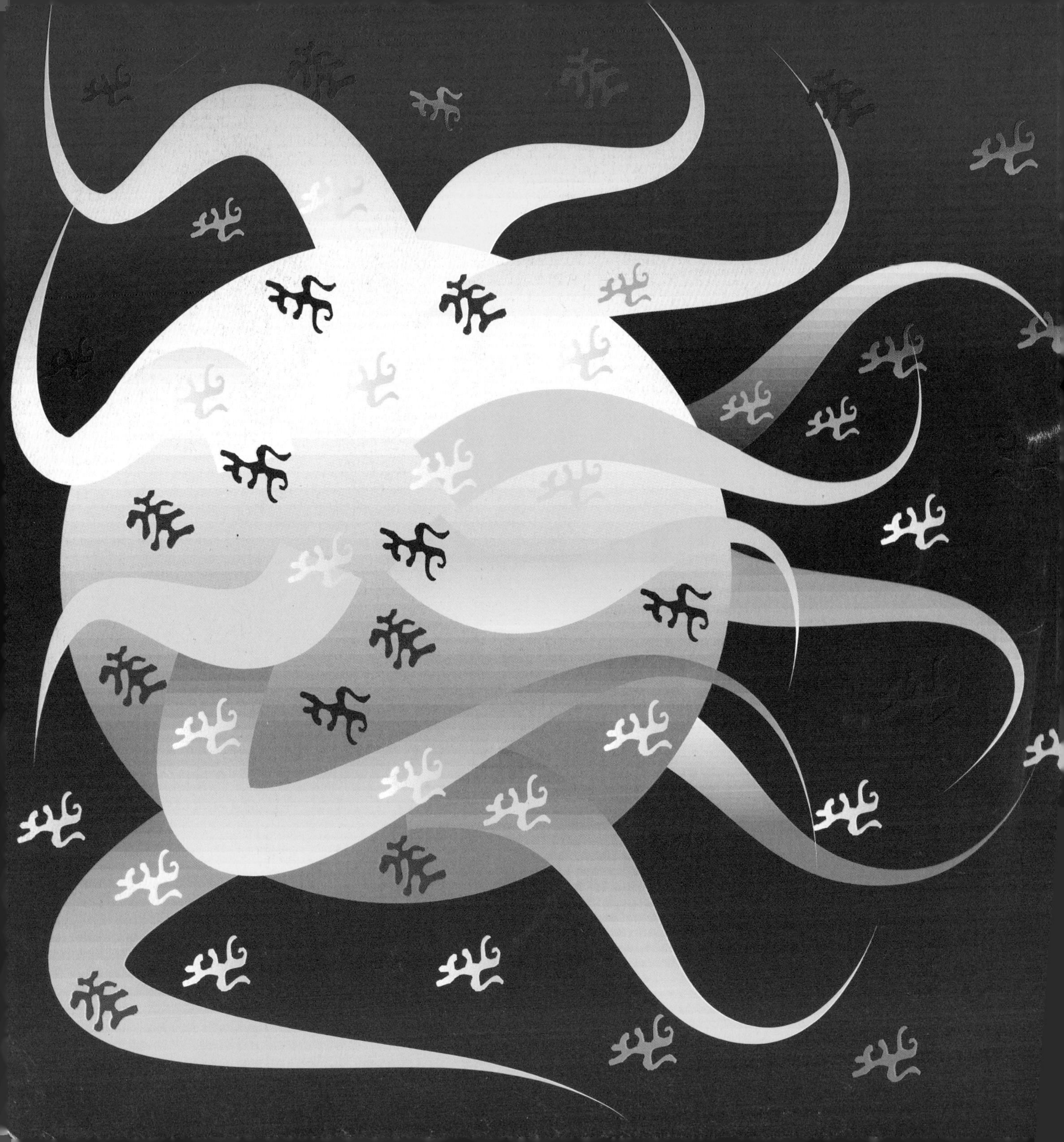

Once upon a time in the sky there
was only the sun and the moon.

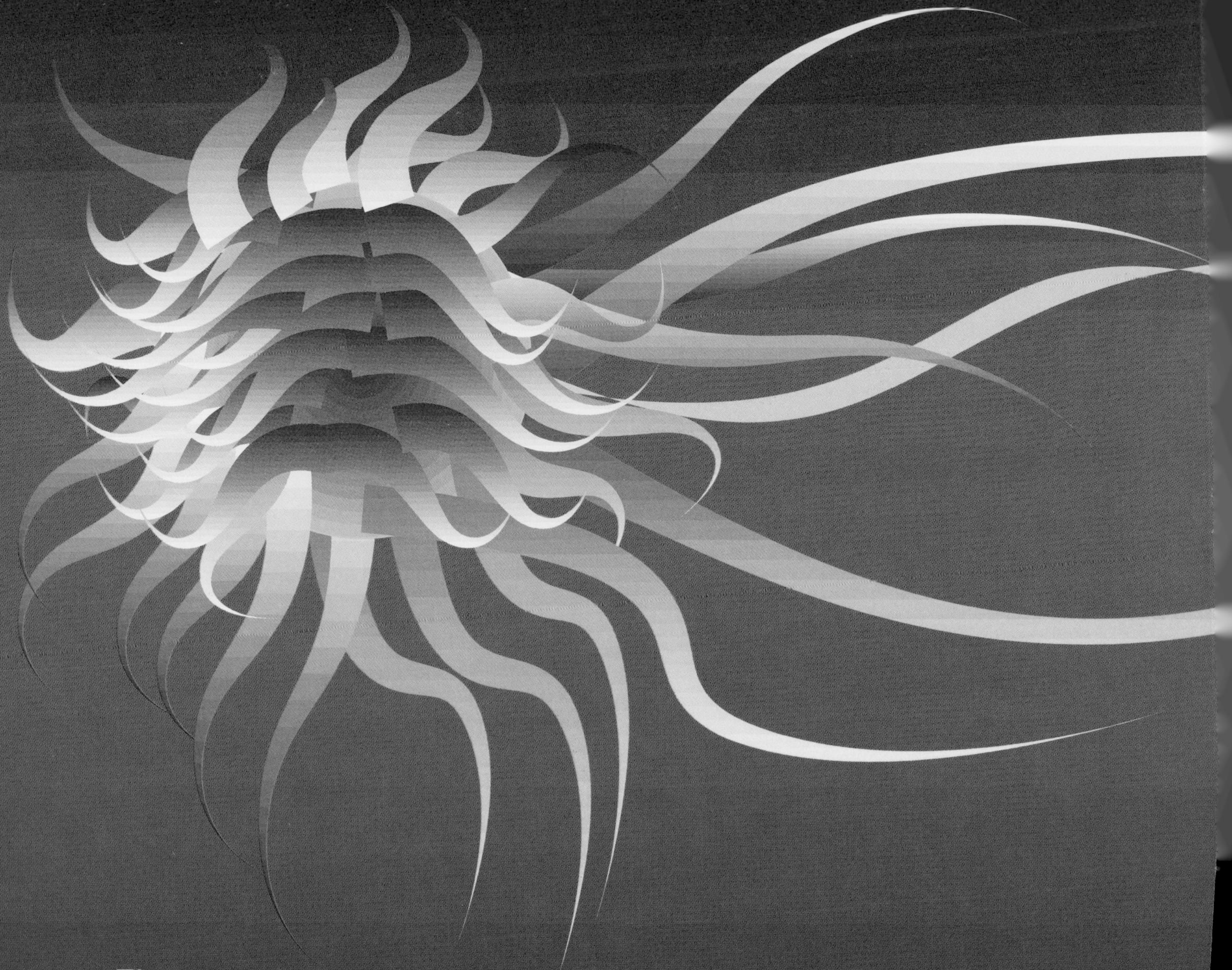

The sun was very, very big and very, very

HOT.

The moon was very, very small and
the man in the moon sat on it.
The man in the moon had nowhere to go
to get away from the blazing heat of the
sun and so he was very, very HOT, too.

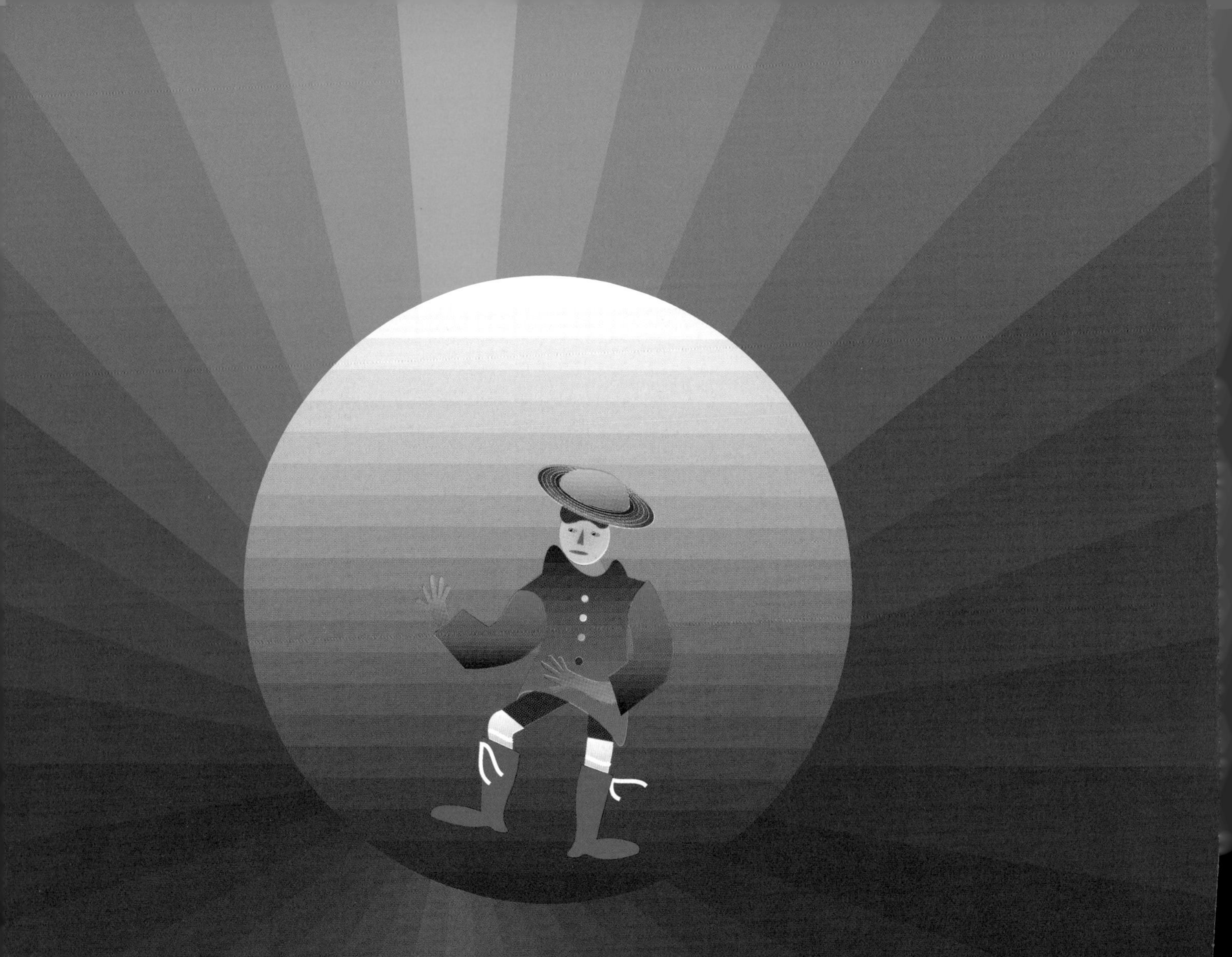

Now the man in the moon had beautiful clothes. He had a lovely hat with a broad colourful brim, big blue boots, wooly grey socks and a most

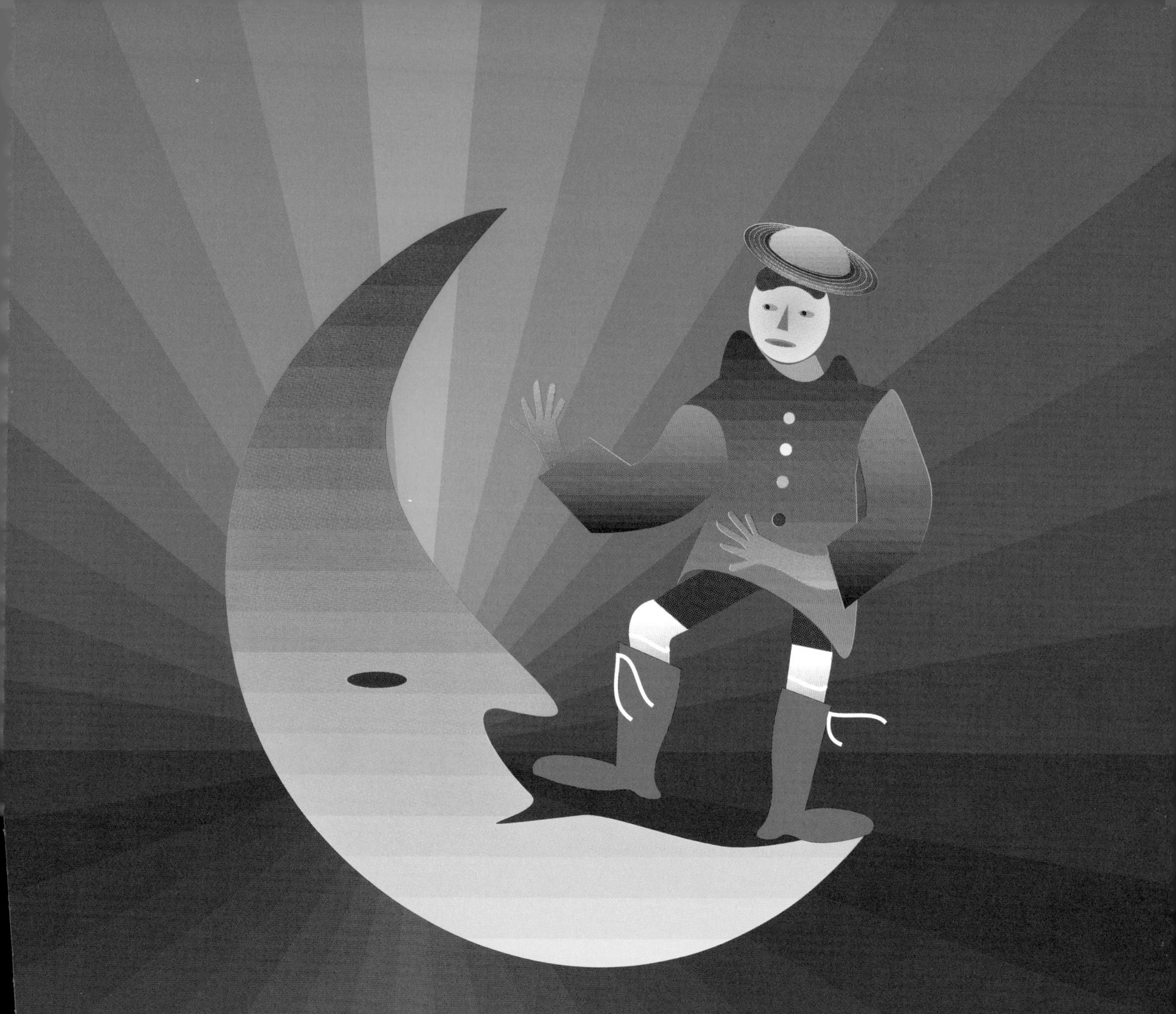

beautiful blue and green coat with coloured buttons. He was very proud of his clothes.

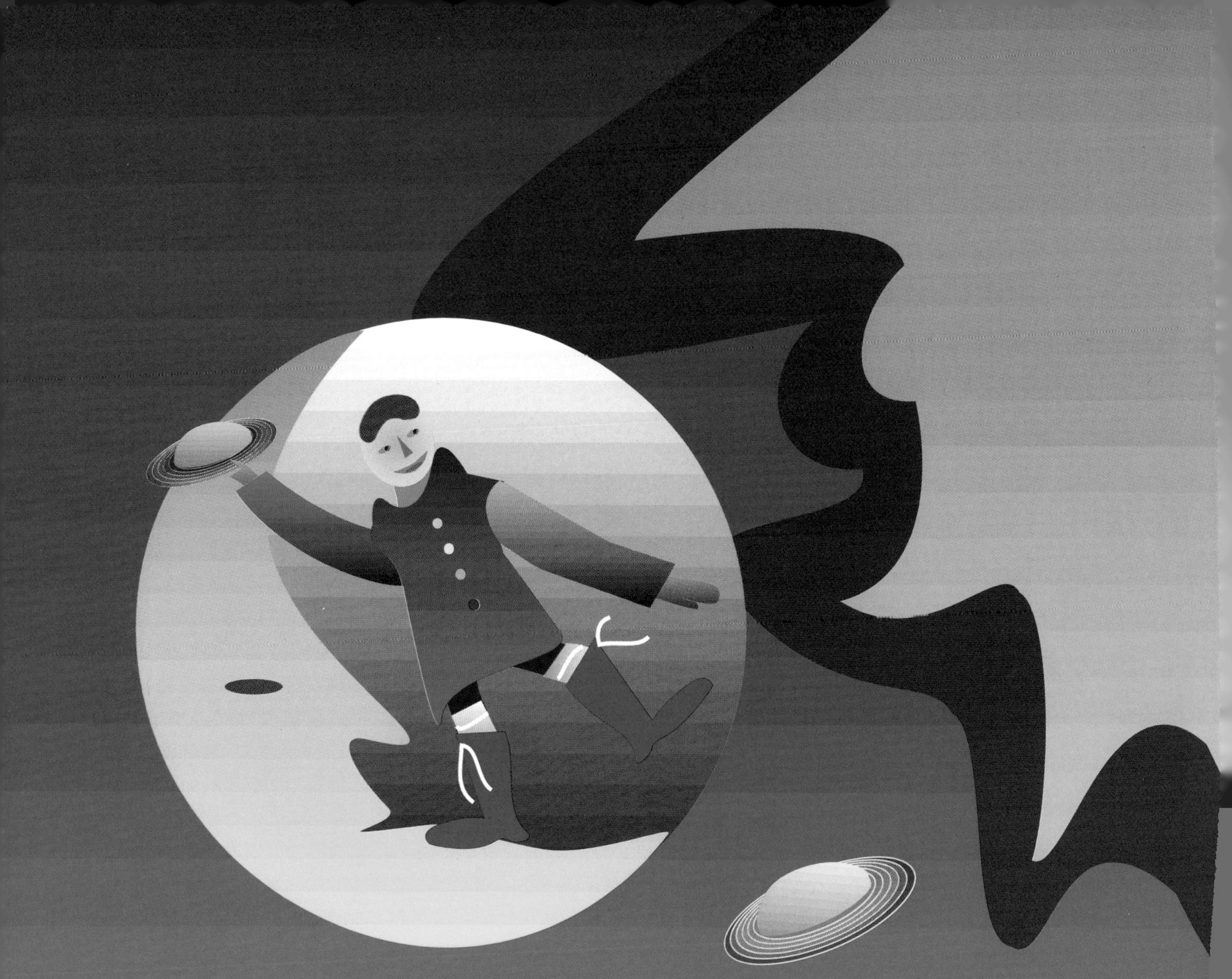

But one day he decided that he was too hot so he took off his lovely hat with the broad colourful brim and threw it into the sky.

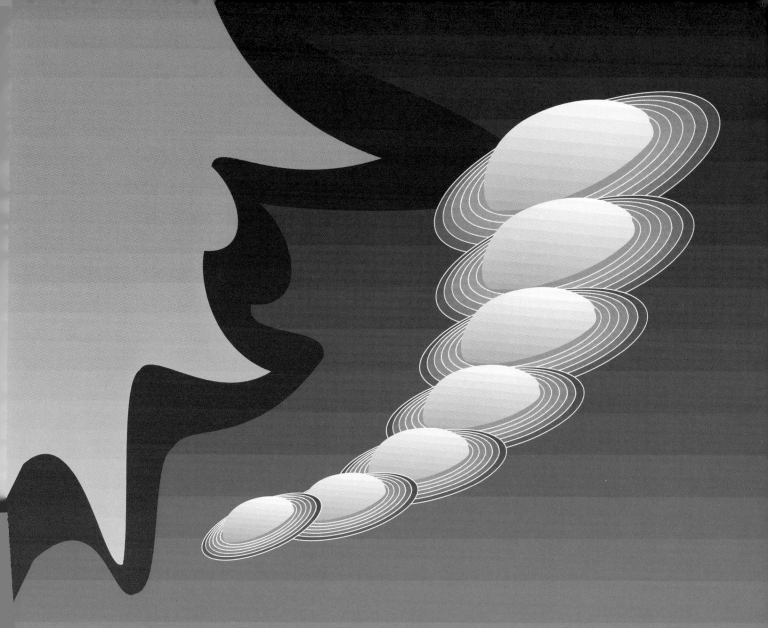

The hat spun up and away and got stuck near the edge of the sky. But the man in the moon was still HOT.

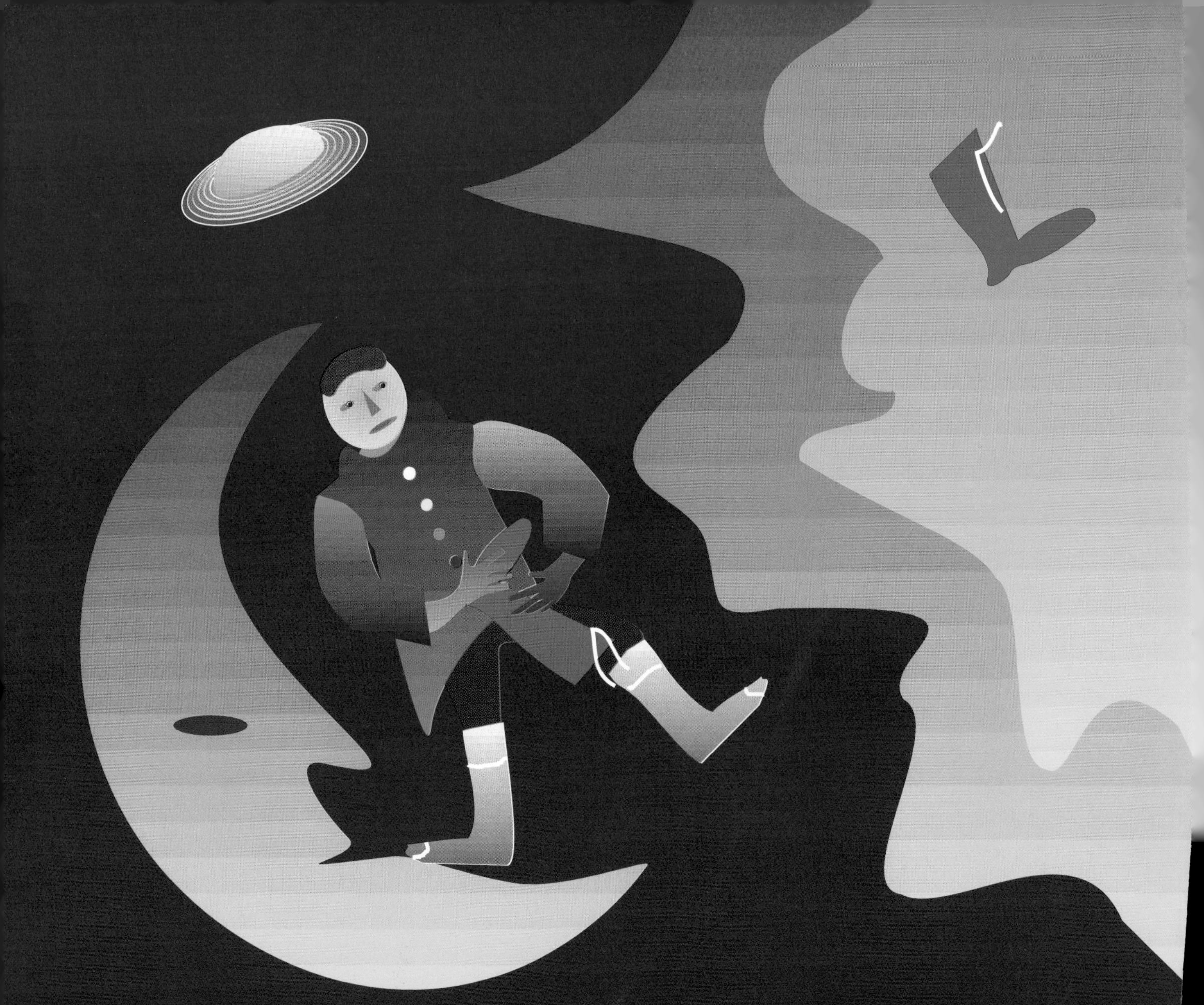

So he took off his big blue boots and
threw them into the sky and they got stuck.

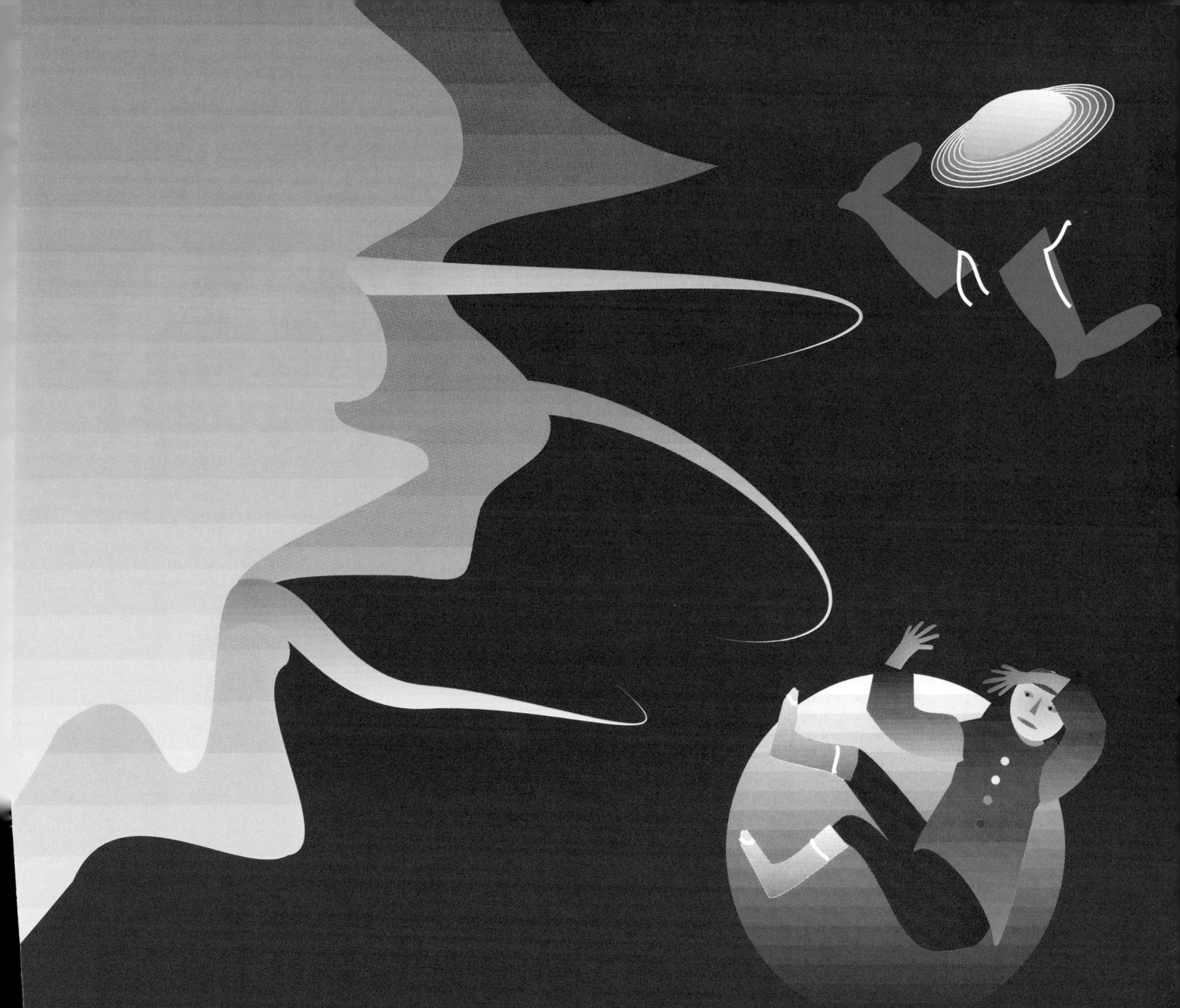

But the man in the moon was still HOT.

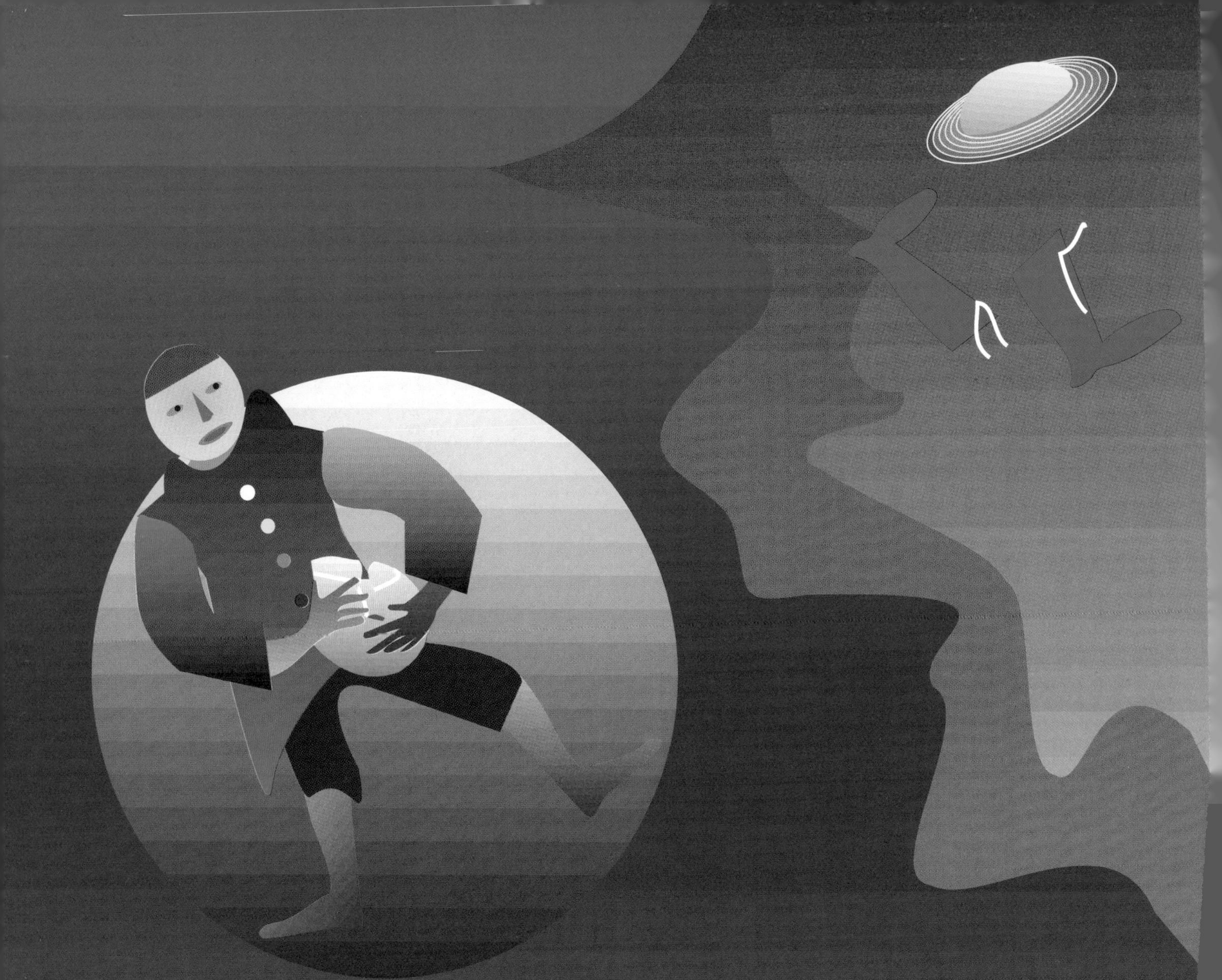

Then he took off his wooly grey socks, rolled them up and tossed them into the sky and they got stuck above his head.

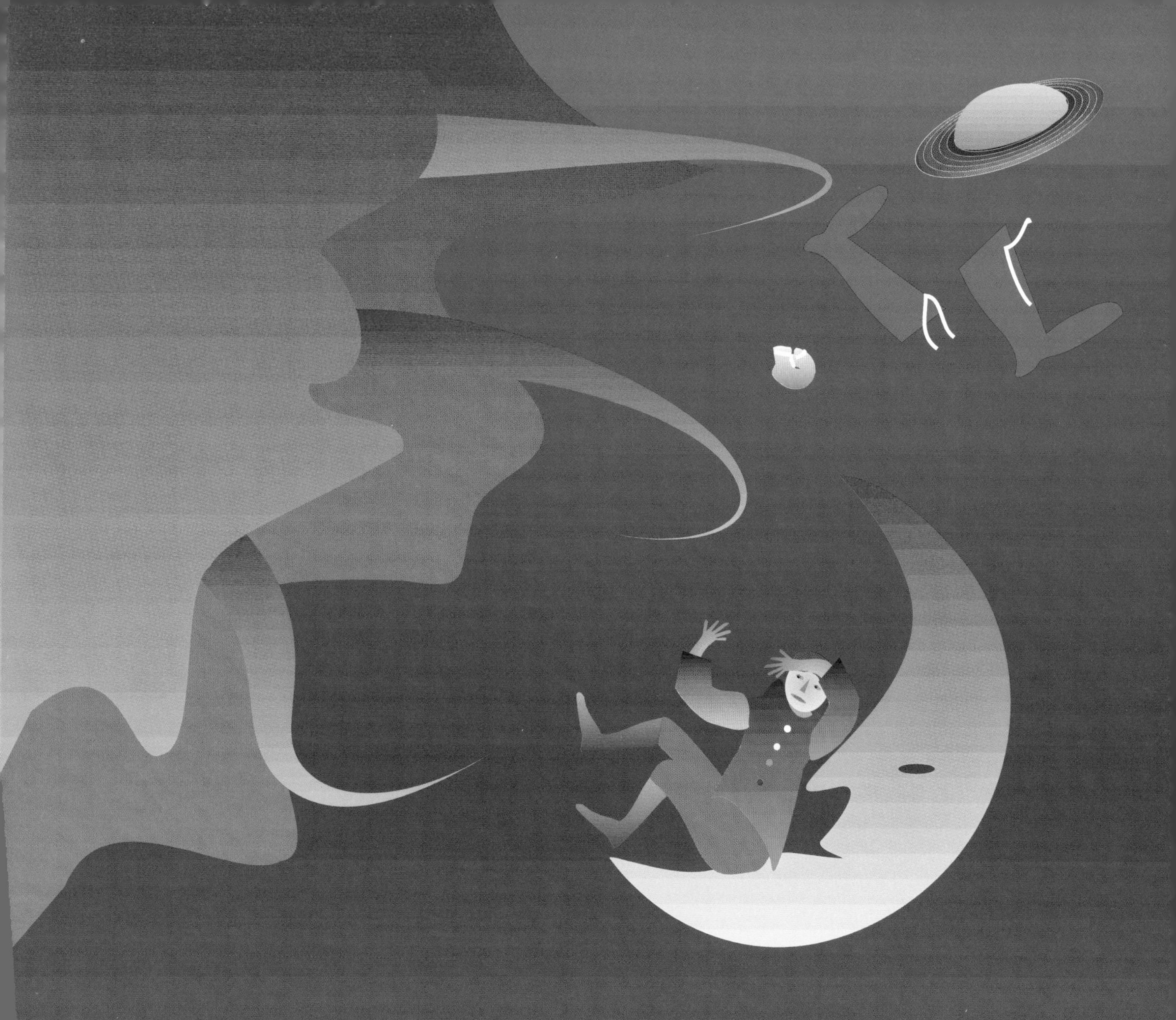

But the man in the moon was still HOT.

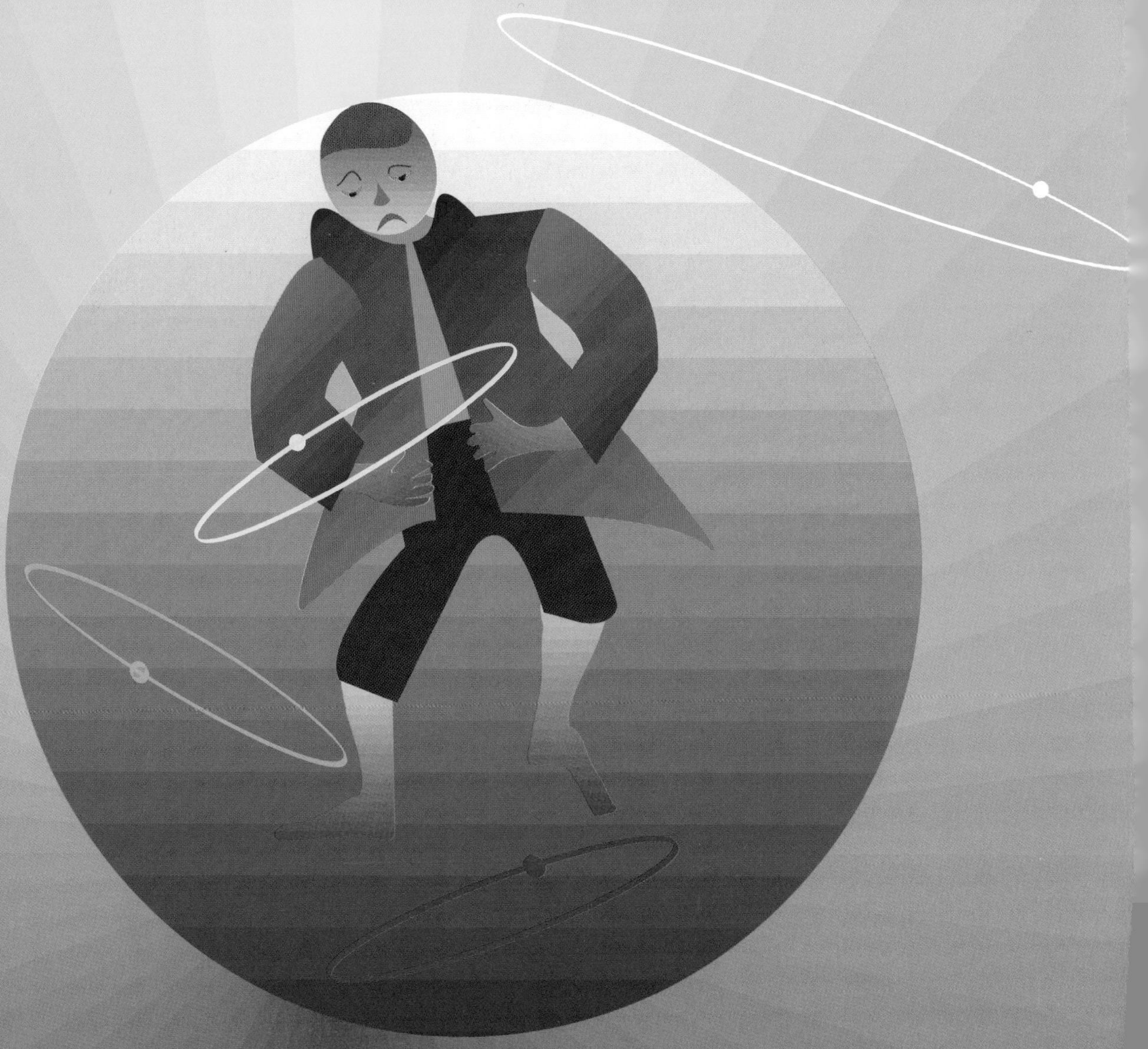

Finally he looked down at his beautiful blue and green coat with the lovely buttons and decided to take it off, but he was careless and the buttons broke off and went spinning into the sky.

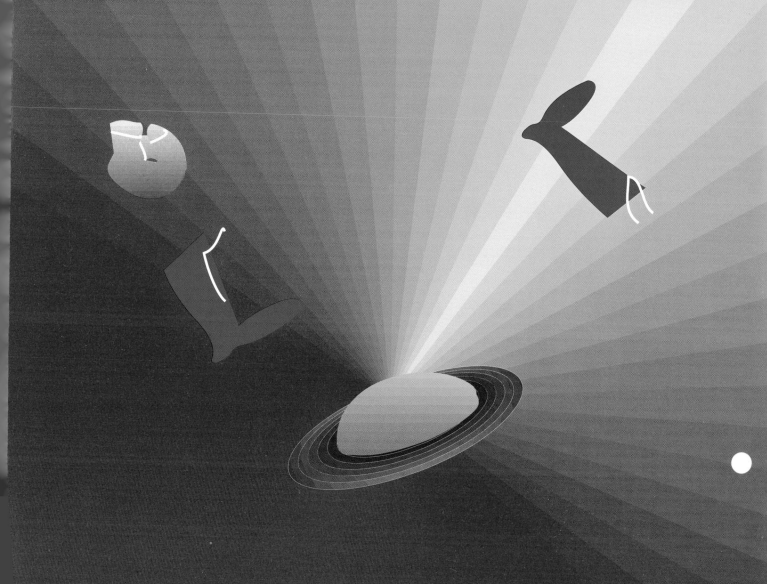

The silver one went way past the wooly grey socks and the big blue boots and the lovely hat with the broad colourful brim and got stuck on the very edge of the sky.

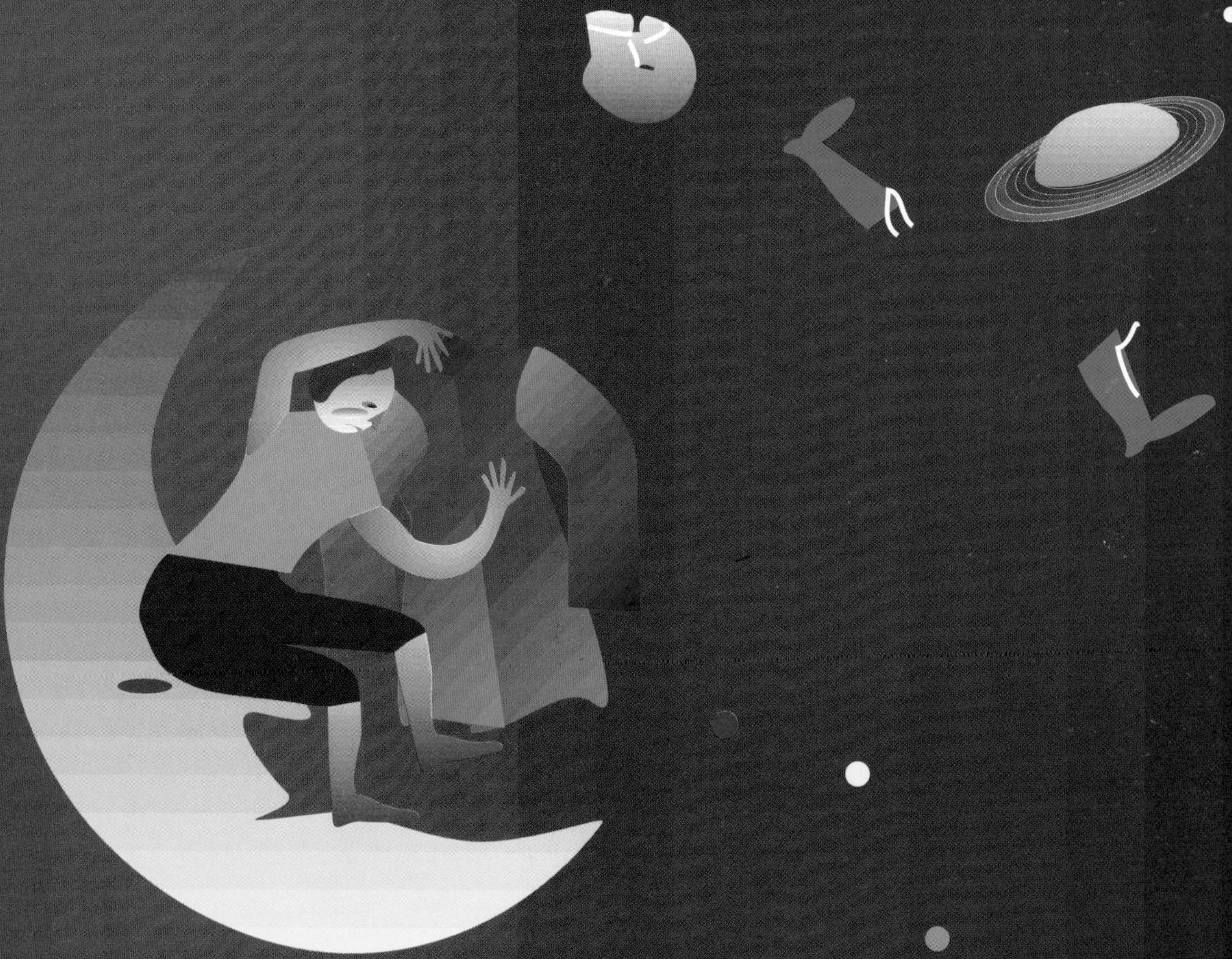

The red, orange and yellow buttons fell towards the sun. The man in the moon was sad. He had lost all his buttons and ruined his beautiful blue and green coat.

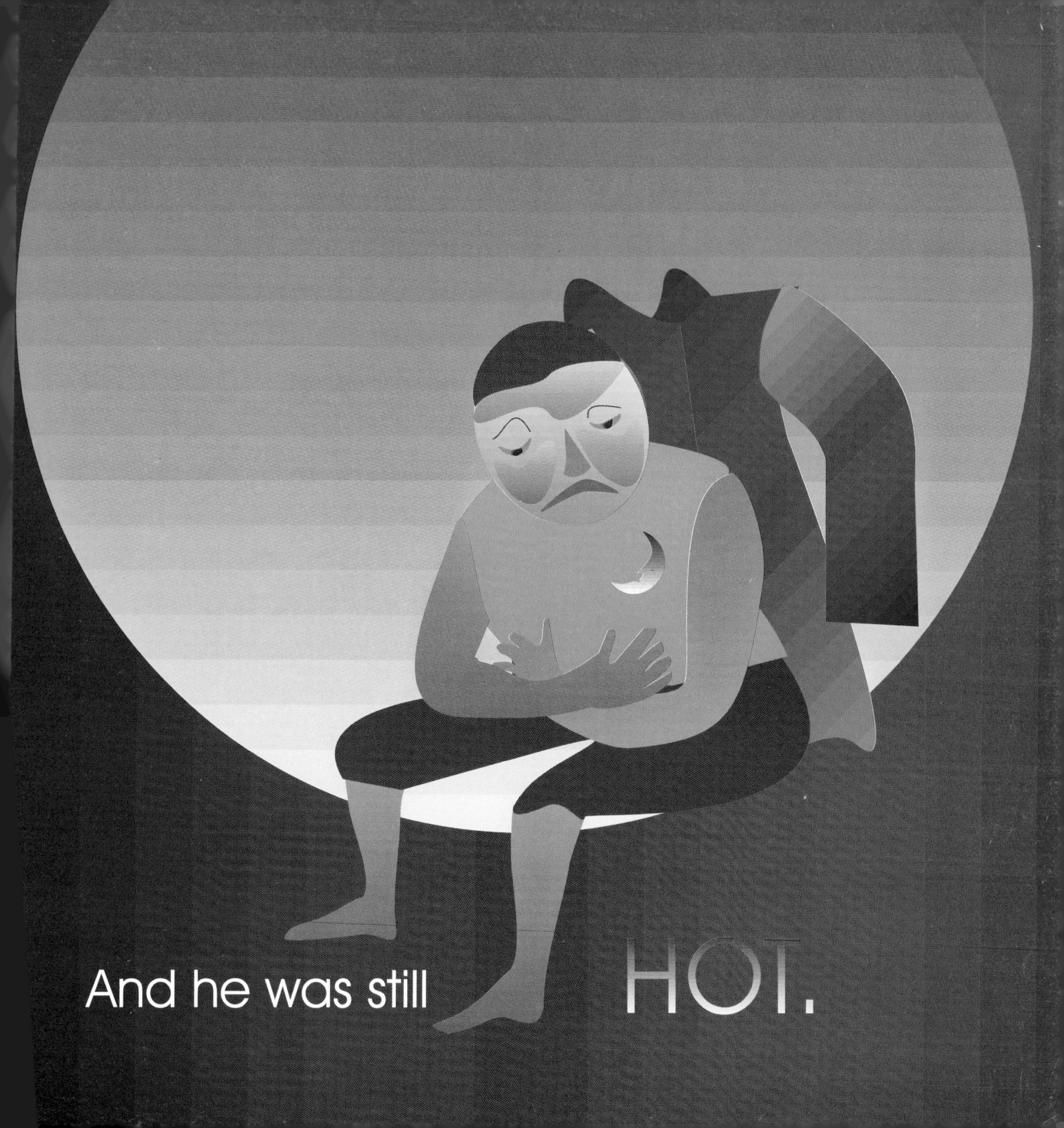

And he was still HOT.

Then the man in the moon saw that as his lovely hat with the broad colourful brim, his big blue boots, his wooly grey socks

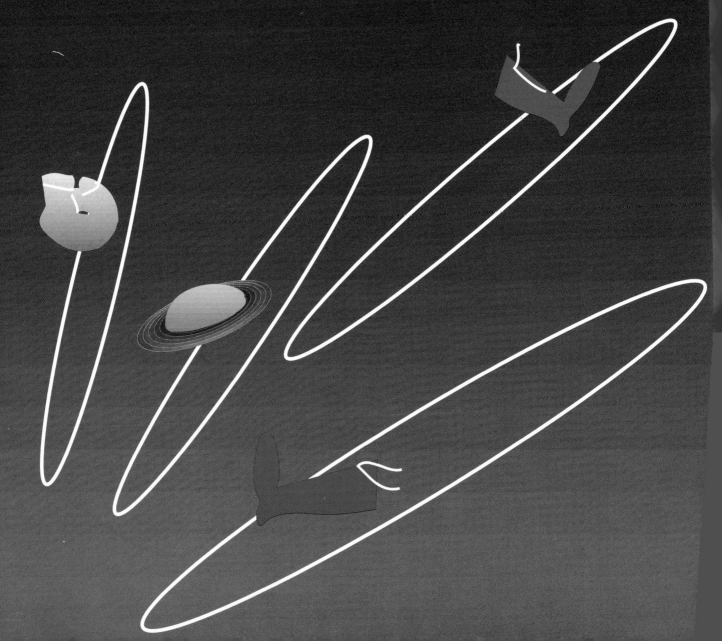

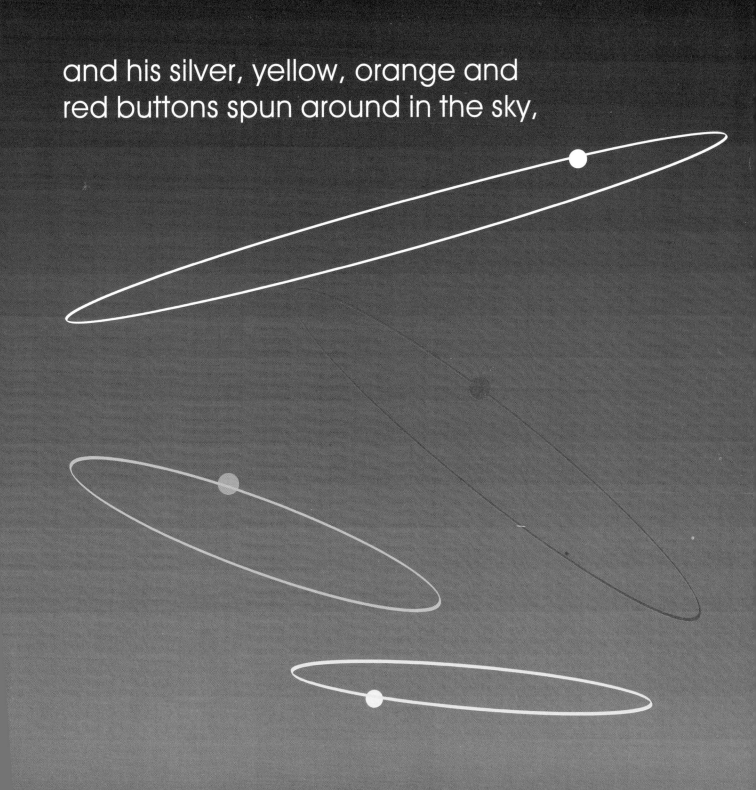

and his silver, yellow, orange and
red buttons spun around in the sky,

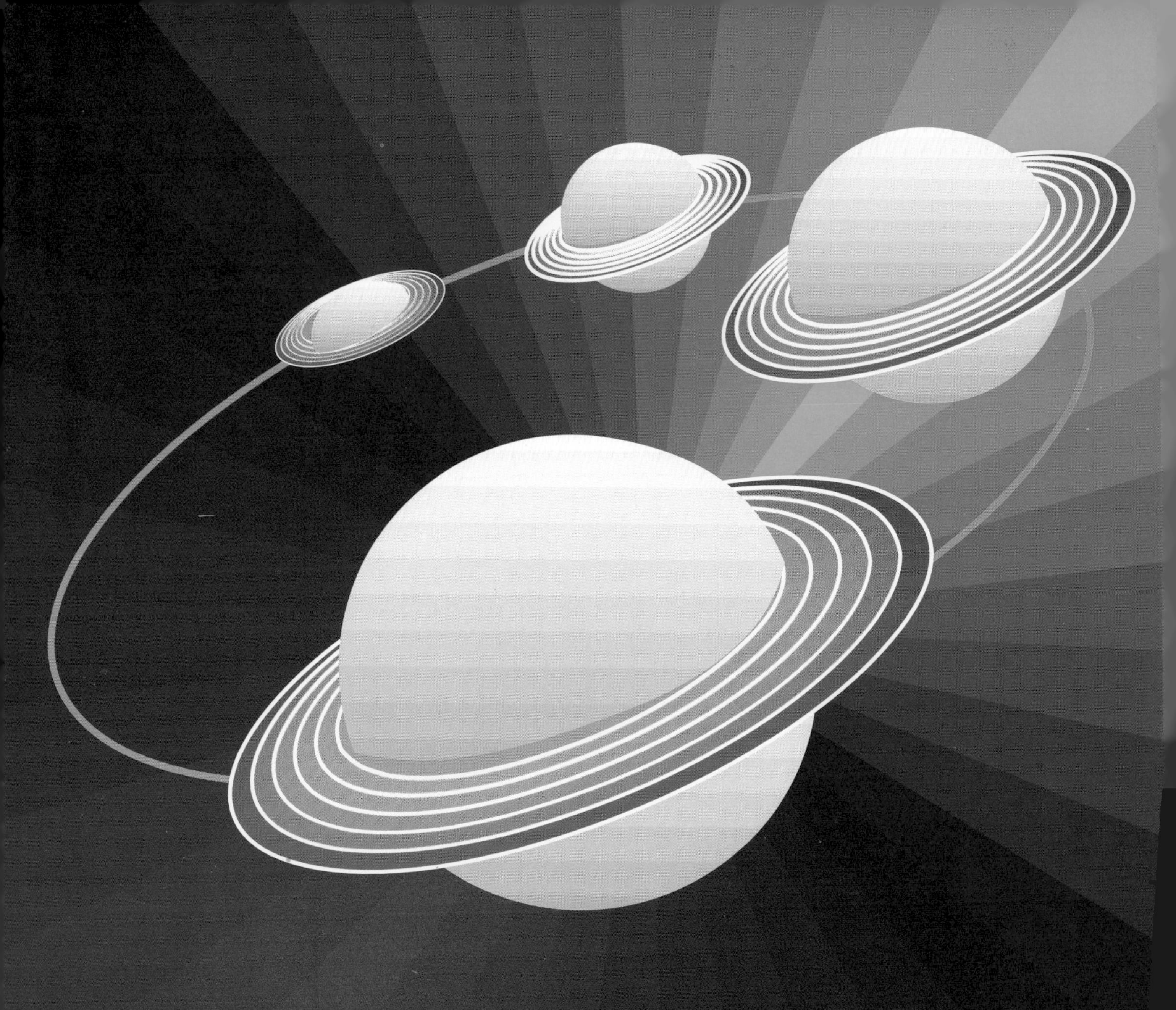

they slowly got bigger and bigger

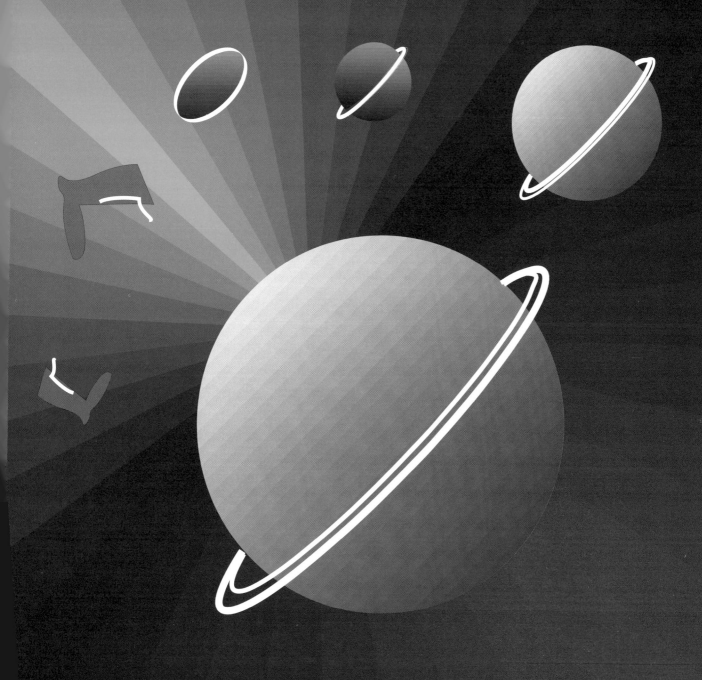

and rounder

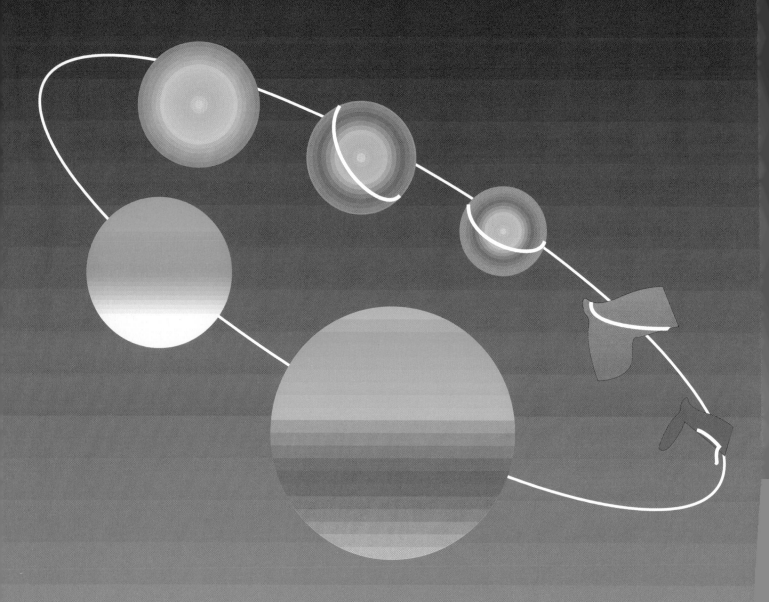

and rounder

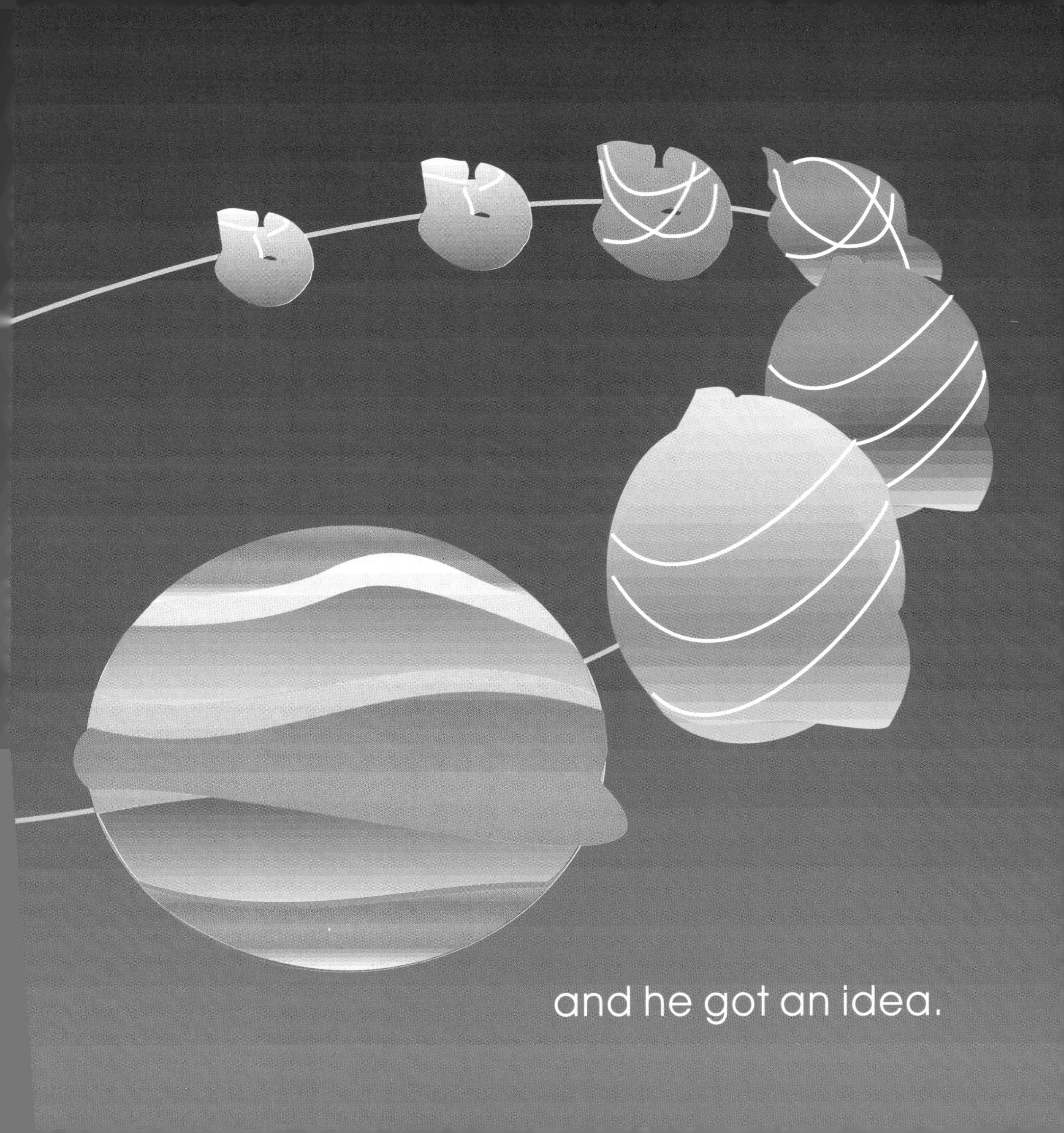

and he got an idea.

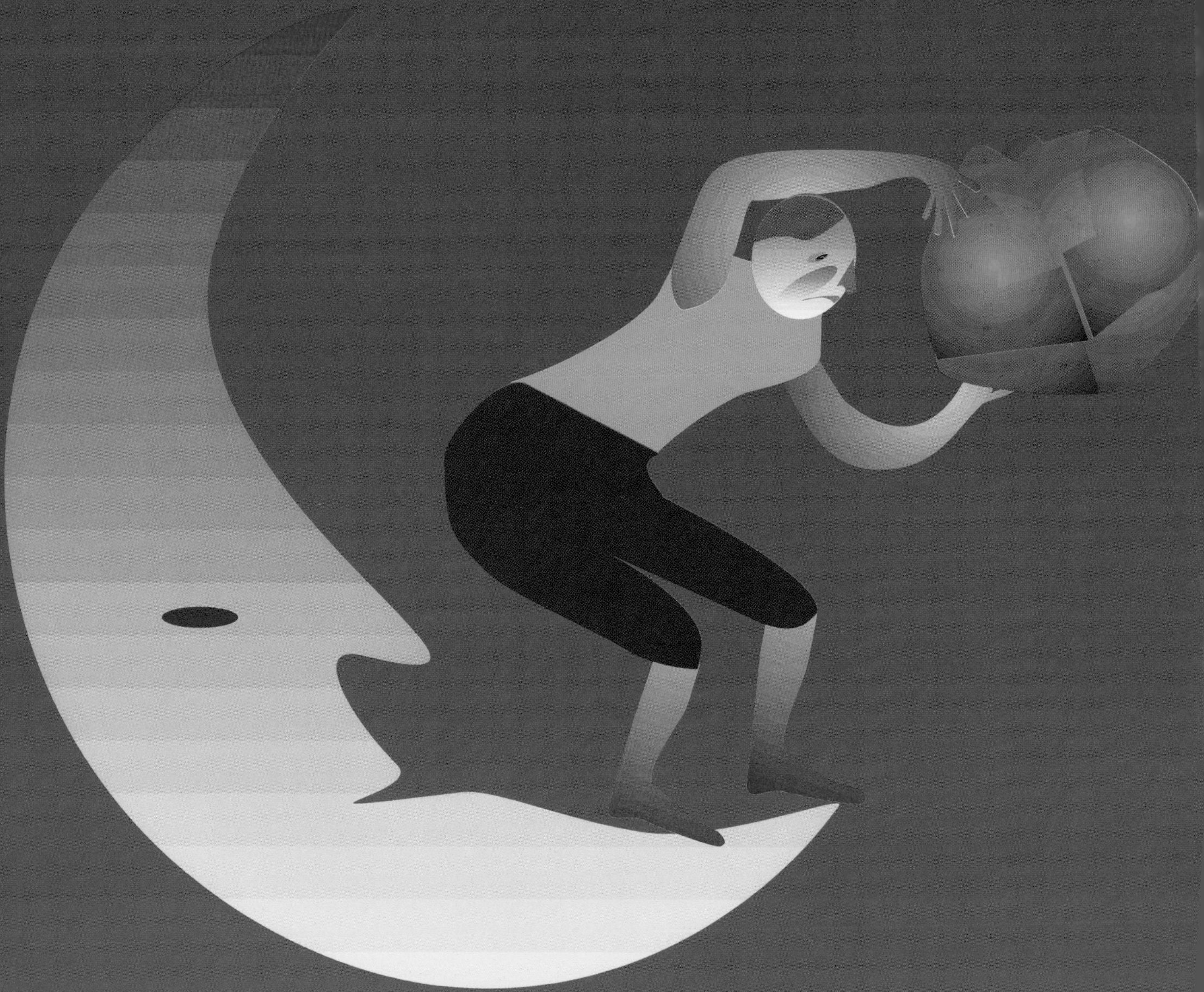

He carefully took his beautiful blue and green coat, rolled it up and stuck it in the sky

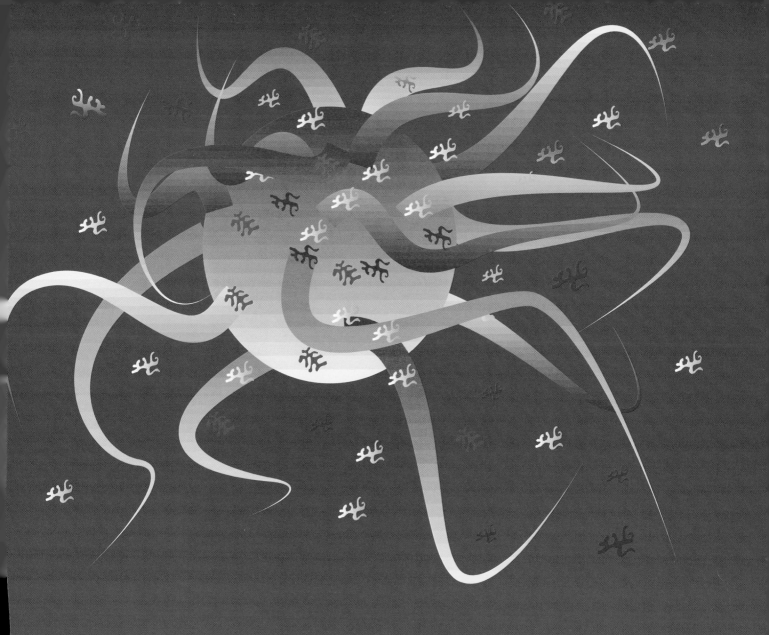

between the sun and the moon.

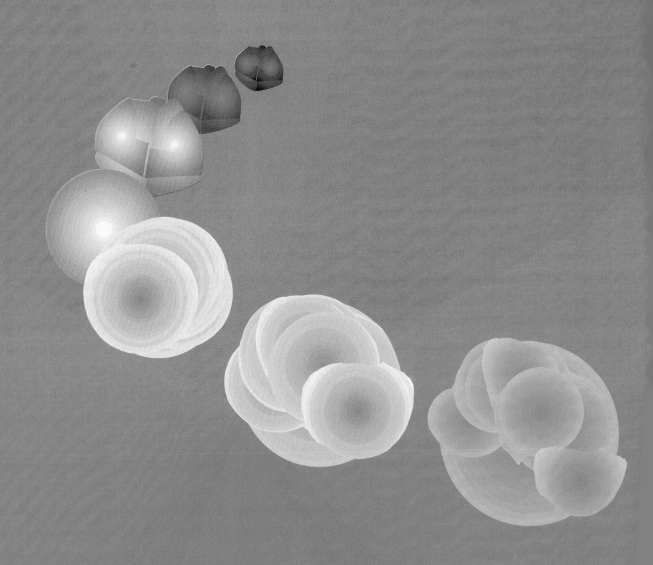

And the coat began to spin and as it spun

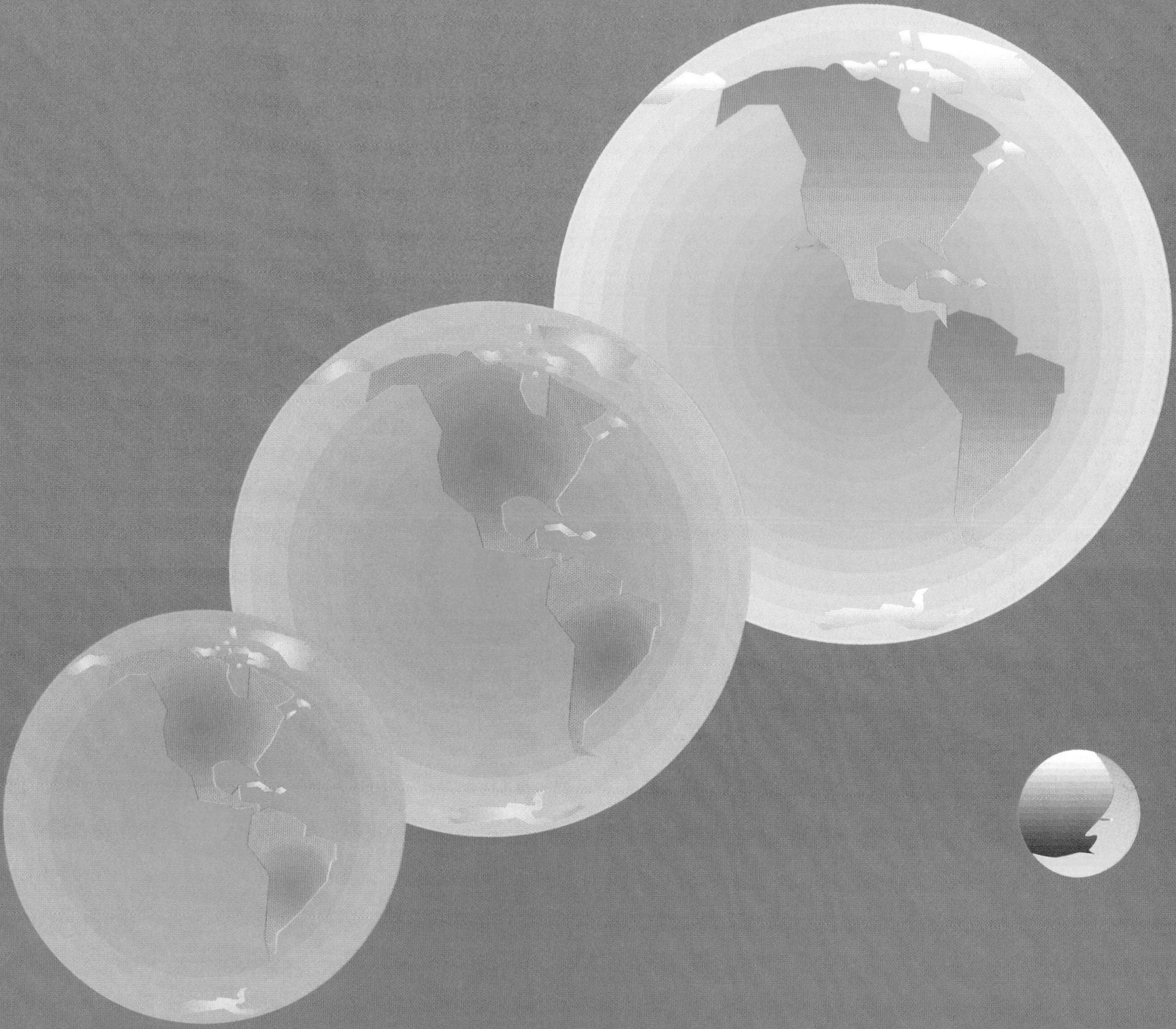

it got bigger and bigger and rounder and
rounder and made a shady place behind it
over the moon.

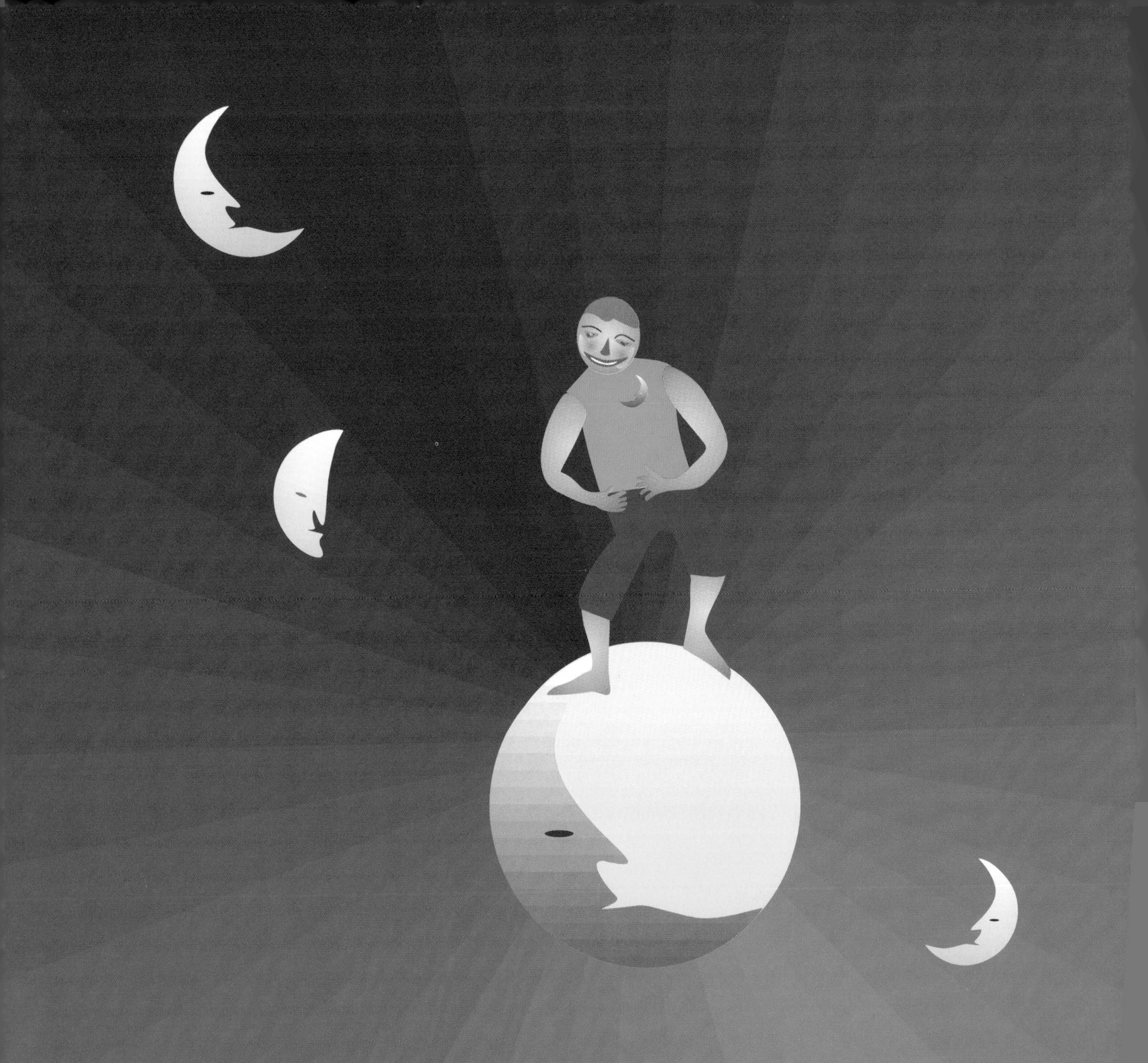

And the man in the moon wasn't hot anymore!

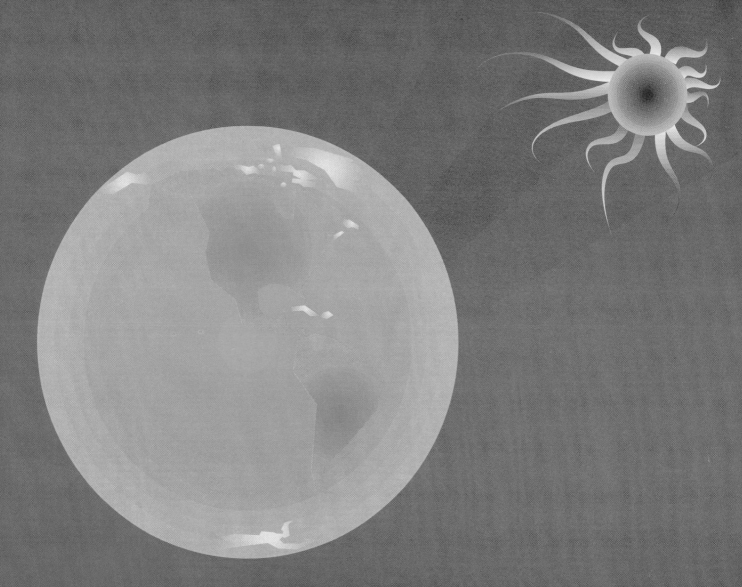

In fact sometimes he felt a little bit cold without his clothes, and then he would wiggle the moon around to the sunny side for a while until he was warm again!

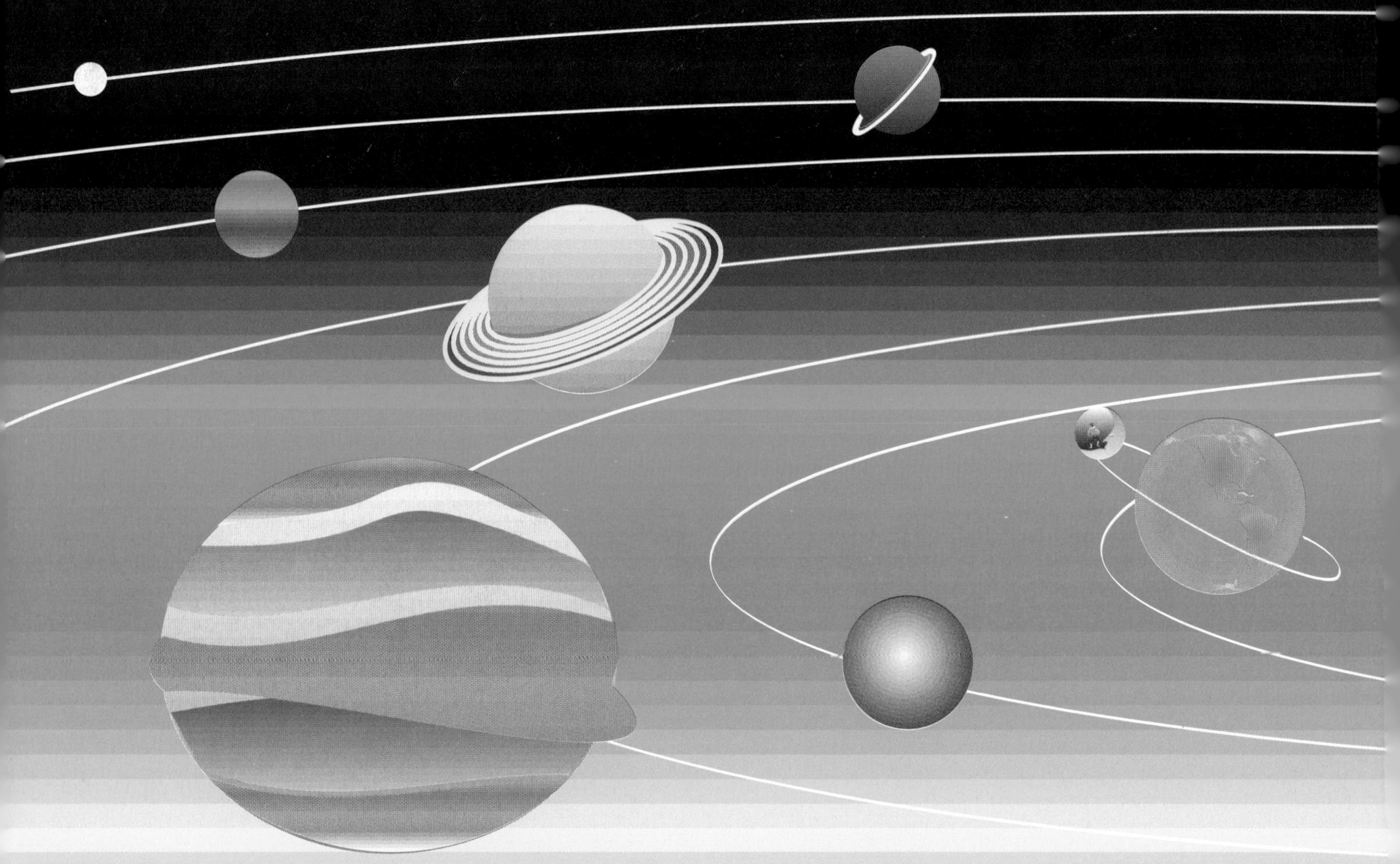

And the man in the moon lived happily ever after an
his lovely hat with the broad colourful brim, his big blue boots, his wooly grey socks, his silver and yellow and orange and red buttons and his beautiful blue and green coat stayed in the sky forever and kept spinning around and around the sun.

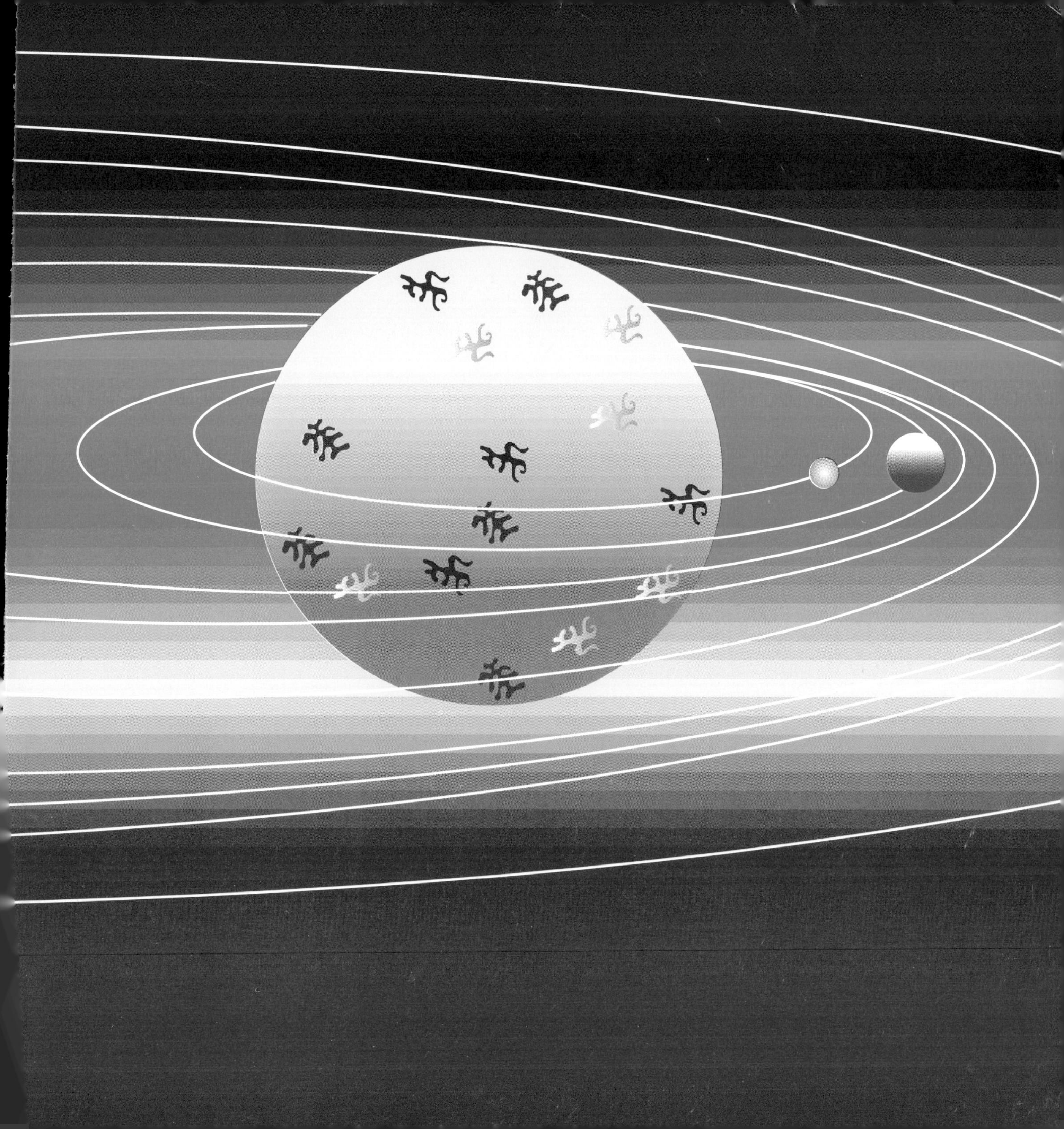

For Jane who prompted this idea,
with love and thanks, Mum.

Text copyright © 1998 by Diane Brookes

Illustrations copyright © 1998 by Ann Timmins

Published in Canada by Raven Rock Publishing, Yellowknife, NWT
21 Burwash Drive, Yellowknife, NT X1A 2V1

PRINTED IN CANADA BY ARTISAN PRESS LTD

Canadian Cataloguing in Publication Data

Brookes, Diane
  The man in the moon

ISBN 0-0-9683234-0-5

1. Solar system – Juvenile fiction. I. Timmins, Ann 1952- II.
Title.   jC813'.54   C98-910162-2
PS8553.R6546M36 1998
PZ7.B78979Ma 1998